Chloe

Everyone who's good at something
has got a best friend, thought Chloe.
That was what she wished for more
than anything – a very best friend…

D0684284

For Holly Pilkington, who read this first

ORCHARD BOOKS
96 Leonard Street, London EC2A 4XD
Orchard Books Australia
Unit 31/56 O'Riordan Street, Alexandria, NSW 2015
First published in Great Britain in 2002
A PAPERBACK ORIGINAL
Text © Ann Bryant 2002
Series conceived and created by Ann Bryant
Series consultant Anne Finnis
The right of Ann Bryant to be identified as the author
of this work has been asserted by her in accordance with the
Copyright, Designs and Patents Act, 1988.
A CIP catalogue record for this book is available
from the British Library.
ISBN 1 84121 734 4
1 3 5 7 9 10 8 6 4 2
Printed in Great Britain

Make Friends With Chloe

Ann Bryant

ORCHARD BOOKS

Chapter One

In Chloe's bedroom the bedcovers were
half on and half off the bed. One of
her pillows was on a chair. The other
was on top of her wardrobe where she
had thrown it. Every single book from
her bookcase was on the floor, because
she'd tipped them all out. She'd thrown
her toys all over the carpet as well. And
right in the middle of this mess, sat
Chloe, hunchbacked and grumpy.

It's not fair, she thought. Everyone's

good at something except me. I'm the only person in my whole class who's not good at anything at all. I can't even play the recorder without it squeaking.

She got up and looked out of her bedroom window. Her recorder was lying on next door's lovely neat lawn. She had thrown it so hard that it had gone flying over the hedge. But Chloe didn't care.

"I hope the rain comes pouring down and spoils it," she said out loud in a rather gruff voice. "In fact I hope a big dog comes along and wees in all the holes."

Thinking naughty thoughts about the recorder made Chloe feel a bit better. But only a bit.

She frowned as she thought of the girls at school. Then quite suddenly she felt as though she'd worked out the answer to a very difficult sum.

Everyone who's good at something has got a best friend. So if I was good at something, I might get a best friend too! she thought.

That was what Chloe wished for more than anything — a very best friend. She sighed as she went back to sit in the middle of the messy carpet, and spotted her sketch pad poking out from under the bed.

That gave her a brilliant idea. Maybe she could be good at drawing. If she practised hard, she might even get to be the best at drawing in her class. She rummaged around under the bed and found a pencil.

Right, I'm going to draw a horse in a field. She gripped the pencil tightly and started drawing. She always held her breath for ages when she did drawing or writing. Then she let it out very noisily. She couldn't help it. It was just something she did.

When the horse was finished, she looked at it and thought it looked stupid. It didn't look anything like a horse. It looked like a cross between an elephant and a big bird with knobbly knees. Even when she held the picture at arm's length, the horse still looked stupid.

Chloe could feel herself getting crosser and crosser. She was just as useless at drawing as she was at everything else. She ripped the page out of the sketch pad and tore it into tiny shreds. She threw the little bits of paper up in the air, then she tipped every single crayon and felt pen on to the carpet. Amongst the felt pens lay a fat black marker pen. Chloe snatched it up in a temper and wrote on her bedroom wall:

I HATE DRAWING IT STINKS!

Then she jumped because she could hear footsteps. She froze. It was her mum coming up the stairs. Any minute now she would come into Chloe's room and see the lovely yellow wall all covered in gigantic black words. Chloe dropped the pen and stared in horror at what she'd done.

Her mum would go absolutely mad when she saw it. And if her dad saw it… he'd probably turn purple with rage. Chloe bit her lip and wondered what on earth to do. Then she remembered

Sophie's birthday party.

Oh no! I'll never be allowed to go to that now, she thought.

❀ ❀ ❀

Chapter Two

Chloe knew she had to get out of the bedroom quickly and stop her mum from going in. She rushed on to the landing, shutting the bedroom door behind her.

"What are you doing, Chloe?" asked her mum, frowning.

"Nothing."

"Well can you move, please, so that I can take these clothes into your room?"

"It's all right, I'll take them in," Chloe offered.

"No, love. There are some things for you, some for Ben and some for Dad and me."

Ben was Chloe's sixteen-year-old brother. Chloe spotted her green trousers in the middle of the pile. She started trying to yank them out.

"Don't do that. You'll make me drop the whole pile. Open the door and then I can put your things on your bed."

"No, you can't come in."

"Why not? Just open the door, Chloe and stop being silly."

"There's a secret in my room. It's a surprise… It's for you."

Her mum stopped frowning for a moment. *Good*, thought Chloe. *She believes me.* But the suspicious look came back on her mum's face a moment later.

"What sort of a surprise? It's not

my birthday."

"I can't tell you. It's a secret."

"Well you'll just have to hide the surprise and then I can come in with your ironing."

"I can't hide it."

"Why not?"

"Because it's too big."

Her mum sighed. "So when do I get to see this wonderful surprise?"

Chloe just said the first thing that came into her head.

"Tomorrow."

Her mum pursed her lips. She did not look happy. She left Chloe's things outside her bedroom door.

"Go and put these clothes away then. We're going out to buy Sophie her birthday present, remember."

Now it was Chloe's turn to frown.

Although she really wanted to go to Sophie's party, she did feel rather nervous about it, because Sophie was very bossy. She showed off a lot too, but that was no wonder, because she was so good at everything.

Never mind, she won't be able to be bossy and showy-offy with her mum there, thought Chloe.

When Chloe had put her clothes away, she wrote a sign and stuck it on her bedroom door.

Big surprise in here. Nobody allowed in or you will spoil the surprise.

Chloe planned to clean her wall as soon as she got back from buying Sophie's present. She thought that if she got a cloth and some soap, and if she rubbed hard enough, the black pen would be sure to come off. She picked up the pen and read what it said on it. *PERMANENT MARKER.*

Little goose bumps came out all over Chloe. That word 'permanent' meant that the black pen would not come off. It would be there on her wall for ever!

❀ ❀ ❀

Chapter Three

Chloe's mum set off at a brisk pace.

"Come on, don't dawdle. I've got a lot to do today."

Chloe was trying to peer through the gap in the hedge at the front of next door's garden. She wanted to see her recorder.

"What *are* you doing, Chloe? Mrs Baxter might be looking, you never know. It's very rude to stare into people's windows."

Chloe was about to tell her mum
that she wasn't staring into the windows,
she was looking at the garden. But she
decided not to say anything. She didn't
think her mum would be too pleased if
she found out that Chloe had thrown her
recorder into Mrs Baxter's garden.

Mrs Baxter lived on her own and
Chloe didn't see her very often. She once
saw her gardening though. She was
kneeling down on a cushion and pulling
out weeds. She had neat silver hair and
a soft wrinkly face.

Chloe knew she was going to have
to find a way to get her recorder back
from Mrs Baxter. Maybe she could tell
her mum that it had just dropped out
of the window and the wind blew it over
the hedge. Perhaps if her mum thought
it was an accident she'd go round to

Mrs Baxter's herself and ask for the recorder back. Really, Chloe knew this was silly. After all, the recorder couldn't jump over into Mrs Baxter's garden on its own. It would take a hurricane to blow it up in the air and over the hedge.

Chloe sighed a big sigh and wished again that she didn't keep doing stupid things in a big temper. If only she could be good at something maybe she wouldn't get so cross all the time.

"What do you think Sophie would like for her birthday," said Chloe's mum when they came to the shops.

Chloe thought about Sophie's pink and purple bedroom. It was so full of toys and things you could hardly fit the bed in.

"Don't know," said Chloe, a bit grumpily.

"What about a book?" suggested her mum.

"A book!" said Chloe, pulling a face. "I don't think so."

"I bet if we get her a book about horses she'll like it," her mum replied.

Chloe wasn't sure. She had the feeling that Sophie might think all books were stupid. It would be awful if she opened Chloe's present and said something horrible about it in front of everyone.

Inside the bookshop there were lots of books about horses. Some of them had got hard backs and lovely shiny pictures in them. There was one that was bigger than all the others. The moment Chloe saw it, she felt quite certain that Sophie would think it was brilliant.

"Let's get this one," she said to her mum.

"It's a bit expensive, Chloe."

"I'll help pay with my pocket money."

"No, it's all right. We can just about afford it. But don't you think Sophie might prefer a book with a story?"

Chloe shook her head. She was imagining the look on Sophie's face when she opened the present and saw the lovely, big, glossy book.

A nice warm feeling was spreading right through Chloe's body. She couldn't wait to get to the party now.

✿ ✿ ✿

Chapter Four

The moment Chloe and her mum got home, Chloe rushed upstairs. She knew it was impossible, but she was hoping that a miracle might have happened while she'd been out. Before she went into her bedroom she shut her eyes and said a magic spell in a witchy voice:

"Abracadabra, izzy wizzy woo,
Make Chloe's wall as good as new!"

Then she opened her eyes and flung open the bedroom door. Immediately a big feeling of disappointment came rushing over her. The writing was still there, just as bold and black as ever.

Chloe knew what she had to do. She sneaked into the bathroom and found the bathroom cleaner by the bath. There was a J-cloth there too. She soaked it in warm water then squeezed it out and went back into her bedroom. She shut the door firmly and set to work.

Going round and round in circles and pressing as hard as she could, Chloe rubbed away at the I HATE bit. But a terrible thing was happening. The letters were turning into huge dark grey smudges. The wall looked worse than ever.

She stopped rubbing and sat on the carpet wondering what on earth to do now. Her heart was beating loudly. She stared round the bedroom, and suddenly a brilliant idea came into her head. If she moved her chest of drawers against that bit of wall, it would hide the writing. But better than that, she could say that this was the big surprise she'd got for her mum. *Yes!*

It took ages to get all the clothes out of the chest. Next Chloe had to take the drawers out so the chest wouldn't be too heavy. The room looked as though a bomb had exploded right in the middle of it. There was so much mess everywhere. Never mind. It would soon be perfectly tidy.

She heaved the chest with all her might, and then stared in amazement because it had fallen over and landed with a crash on the floor. She hadn't expected it to be so light.

"What ARE you doing up there,

Chloe?" came her mum's voice from the stairs.

"Nothing."

"I'm coming in to have a look, surprise or no surprise."

"No, you'll spoil everything. I tipped my chair over, that's all."

"Hm," said her mum from just the other side of the bedroom door.

Chloe held her breath and waited. She could imagine her mum frowning. A few seconds later she heard footsteps going downstairs.

"Phew! That was a close one!" she muttered as she awkwardly lifted the chest of drawers. This time she pushed it gently until it was against the wall. Then a big grin spread over her face. The chest was exactly the right size to hide the letters. Brilliant!

Chloe set about tidying the rest of her bedroom next. It was quite good fun now that she knew her terrible mistake had been covered up. She sang to herself as she put the drawers back in the chest and the clothes back in the drawers. She placed her felt pens and crayons all pointing in the same direction in their box. She arranged her books on the bookcase with the small ones on the top shelf and the big ones on the bottom. She put her toys and things away. She even straightened the rug and pulled the curtains back until they hung in a straight line.

"All spick and span!" said Chloe, going out of her room and closing the door behind her. "The surprise is ready now, Mum!" she called from the landing.

"That was quick," said her mum as

she came upstairs. "I thought you said tomorrow."

"It didn't take as long as I thought," said Chloe truthfully. Then she opened her door.

"Da-daa!"

Chloe watched her mum's face. A puzzled look was spreading over it.

"I think I must have come into the wrong bedroom," she said. "This can't be MY daughter's bedroom. Chloe Brown is not THIS tidy!"

Chloe giggled because her mum was joking.

"I've moved my chest, see?"

"Ye-es," said her mum, looking a bit doubtful. "What made you decide to move it? It must have been very heavy."

"I just wanted a change around, that's all."

"It looks lovely. Well done."

Her mum gave her a hug, then they went down to have some lunch.

As Chloe followed her mum downstairs she began to feel a bit guilty. She should have been feeling perfectly happy, because she'd escaped a big telling-off. But for some reason or other she didn't feel very happy at all. It was as if her naughtiness hadn't really gone away. It was still hiding behind the chest of drawers.

✿ ✿ ✿

Chapter Five

After lunch Chloe helped her mum wrap up Sophie's present. Then she wrote in the birthday card:

Love from Chloe

"Shall I go and get changed now, Mum?" she asked. She was getting impatient for ten to three to come. That's when they were going to set off.

"As long as you don't get your smart clothes messed up. Are you going to wear your lovely blue and white dress?"

Chloe pulled a face.

"Nobody wears dresses any more. I'll wear my blue leggings and my starry top."

"What! For a party!" said her mum. "You'll look so much prettier in your dress, Chloe."

Chloe wondered what Sophie would be wearing. She wanted to be dressed exactly the same. It was true that Sophie had worn a beautiful red dress with lots of stiff petticoats that made it stick out at the school party. Maybe her mum was right. The blue and white silky dress had a belt of white lace, and Chloe thought it was almost as pretty as Sophie's red one.

Of course Sophie had long straight blonde hair which made her look extra nice. Chloe wished her own hair was straight and blonde instead of being curly and boring brown. Chloe had such thick hair that her mum had to use half a bottle of conditioner on it when she washed it, just so that she could get the comb through it.

Chloe sighed as she went up to get changed. If only she had straight blonde hair. Then maybe someone would be her best friend. She would just have to hope that Sophie loved the horse book so much that she didn't mind about having a friend with such frizzy hair.

"You're nearly the last one to arrive," beamed Sophie's mum as she led Chloe into the living room. "I'm just going to pop the sausage rolls into the oven. I'll be back in a minute."

Sophie was sitting on the floor

surrounded by crumpled wrapping paper. She was wearing pink trousers and a purple shiny top. Her hair was twisted into a knot on top of her head and kept in place with a big pink scrunchie. She wore a silver necklace and open-toed sandals. She'd painted her toenails with glittering pink nail varnish, and she was wearing bright pink lipstick.

Chloe suddenly felt babyish in her dress. In front of her mirror at home it had looked so lovely but here it just looked silly. Chloe looked round and her heart sank. She was the only one in a dress. All the other girls were wearing trousers with tight tops.

Sophie didn't even look up when Chloe came in. She just carried on opening her presents, ripping off the paper and chucking it in the air. Everyone laughed when she did that. Chloe sat down in the circle of birthday guests and waited for it to be her turn to give her present. So far no one had given Sophie a book. *Good,* thought Chloe. *That will make my book extra special.*

Just when it was about to be Chloe's turn to give her present, the door opened and in came Sophie's mum. Behind her was a girl who Chloe had never seen before.

"This is Jessica, everyone. She and her family have just moved into a house down the road. She'll be coming to the same school as the rest of you. And I'm sure you'll all look after her because she's new."

Jessica had long blonde hair past her shoulders. Her face looked pale and worried. As Chloe looked at her, she felt a sudden rush of happiness. Jessica was wearing a dress! It was light blue with a dark blue belt. Chloe couldn't help giving her a big smile. Jessica gave a sort of half smile back, as though she was too worried to smile properly.

"Move up, Sophie," said her mum. "Let Jessica sit beside you. That's right. And what about opening Jessica's present now?"

Jessica handed her present over and Sophie had to be reminded to say thank you. She pulled the paper off in two seconds flat. Inside there was a silver bracelet.

"What a lovely present," said Sophie's mum. "Why don't you put it on, Sophie?"

Sophie looked rather bored as she stuck her wrist out for her mum to put on the bracelet.

"Now," said Sophie's mum, jumping up, "I'll just put the chicken nuggets in the oven and then we'll start the games."

Everyone except Chloe and Jessica jumped up excitedly.

"Games! Yeah!" they cried.

Jessica pointed to Chloe.

"You've not opened that girl's present yet," she said softly to Sophie.

"Oh not another one," said Sophie. She sounded as though she'd had so many presents it was getting boring. But she rushed over, all the same, and snatched the present out of Chloe's hands. Then she sat on the settee to open it.

Chloe felt her heart beating fast and her cheeks going pink. She was so excited. Any second now, Sophie would be thanking her for such an absolutely brilliant present. Sophie pulled the book out and hardly glanced at it.

"I've got this one already," she said.
Then she stood up and let the book drop
on to the floor.

Chloe was so disappointed she felt like
crying. Her birthday card was lying on
the floor too. Sophie's mum would
probably scoop it up and put it in the bin.

"Right, everybody, we're going to play
Wink Murder. I'll be the detective first,"
announced Sophie in a bossy voice.

Chloe stood up and even managed a
smile, so no one would know how upset
she was. She wasn't smiling on the inside
though. She was hurting. She wished she
could go home.

❀ ❀ ❀

Chapter Six

After Wink Murder they played Pass-the-Orange-Under-the-Chin, and Guess-the-Animal-Under-the-Blanket.

"Just time for one more game before tea," said Sophie's mum, smiling round.

"Pass the Parcel!" said Sophie firmly. "I want to win the prize!"

"Yes!" cried the others.

"I'm just going to the loo," Chloe told Sophie's mum.

"All right dear. You know where it

is, don't you?"

When Chloe got back into the living room everyone was sitting in a circle playing Pass the Parcel. There wasn't a space in the circle for her to sit though. She was just wondering what to do when the new girl, Jessica, shuffled to the left and patted the floor beside her.

"Come and sit here."

So Chloe sat down next to Jessica, with Sophie on the other side of Jessica.

The game of Pass the Parcel carried on. Sophie's mum was pressing the button on the tape recorder to stop and start the music. She wasn't really paying attention to the game. She was looking out of the window most of the time. But every so often she gathered up the pieces of newspaper that had been ripped off.

The smaller the parcel became, the

faster everyone passed it round. It was very exciting wondering who was going to be the winner and what was going to be the present inside.

"No cheating. You're not allowed to hang on to the parcel," said Sophie, even though nobody was.

But then as soon as it came round to Sophie herself, she took the parcel very slowly and spent ages passing it on. Of course nobody dared to say anything because of Sophie's mum being in the room. Finally so many layers had come off the parcel that everyone felt sure that the very next time the music stopped it would be the last wrapping.

Please let it stop on me, Chloe kept saying over and over again inside her head. The parcel was coming round. It was almost up to Chloe. She felt sure that Sophie's mum would press the stop button just in time. The music had been going on for ages this time.

As Chloe took the parcel, she saw Sophie's mum's hand moving towards the tape recorder. But it was too late. She couldn't hang on to the parcel. That would have been cheating. So she passed it quickly to Jessica and at that very second the music stopped.

Then suddenly Jessica wasn't holding the parcel any more because Sophie had snatched it from her.

"Me! Me!" cried Sophie. "I'm the winner!"

Her mum came over to have a look. "Oh my goodness!" she said, when she saw who had won. "I wasn't paying attention. What a nice surprise for the birthday girl."

Sophie ripped off the paper and took out the present. It was a yellow rucksack with orange stripes down one side of it.

"Wow! Cool!" cried a girl called Gemma.

Then everyone crowded round Sophie. Chloe and Jessica stayed in their places though. They'd had enough of selfish Sophie.

"You can look, but you can't touch," she was saying in her loud, bossy voice.

Nobody was paying any attention to Chloe and Jessica. Suddenly Chloe thought how silly Sophie sounded. She turned to Jessica and said, "Watch this, Jessica." Then she stuck her nose in the air and began to speak in a posh, bossy voice, just like Sophie's: "You can look, but you can't touch."

Jessica burst into giggles. "You sound just like Sophie," she spluttered through her giggles. And that made Chloe giggle too.

✿ ✿ ✿

Chapter Seven

Chloe and Jessica sat next to each other at teatime. Chloe found out that Jessica had a baby brother called Joseph. Jessica found out about Chloe's big brother, Ben. Then they told each other their favourite television programme, favourite colour, favourite food, favourite pop star and lucky number.

"I'm going to ask Mum if you can come and stay over at my house tonight," said Chloe.

"Trouble is, I'm going to stay with my granny tonight while Mum and Dad get the house sorted out a bit," said Jessica. "It's still a mess because we only moved in two days ago. Perhaps I'll be able to come to play tomorrow."

Then Chloe asked Jessica how she knew Sophie.

"I don't really know her," said Jessica. "It's just that our new house is very near Sophie's house, and her mum saw my mum in our front garden, and invited me to the party."

"Time for the cake!" called Sophie's mum.

Everybody sang "Happy Birthday" to Sophie. Then Sophie blew all the candles out on her first puff.

"I guess you're all full," Sophie's mum went on, "So you can each take a slice of cake home with you. Now, how about a video?"

She put one on, then whizzed round the room tidying up.

"What's this?" she suddenly said. Everyone looked round at the same time. Sophie's mum was holding Chloe's present, the horse book. "What's this book doing on the floor, Sophie?"

Sophie went red. "Oh I don't know," she said. "Be quiet, Mum. You're interrupting the video."

Chloe could feel herself getting cross. She'd just about had enough of Sophie Briggs. So had Sophie's mum, because she walked over to the television and switched it off. The room went very quiet.

"Don't be rude, Sophie. Now are you going to tell me where this book came from or not?"

"I don't know where the stupid book came from. I've never seen it before in my life," she snapped at her mother.

Quite a few of the girls gasped. They all looked rather anxious. Chloe was just about to explode with anger when Jessica spoke in a soft voice.

"It was Chloe's present to Sophie, but Sophie said she'd already got it."

It was so quiet after Jessica had spoken that you could have heard a spider spinning its web.

Sophie's mum's lips went into a thin line. She looked as though she was too cross to speak. A moment later though her voice sounded bright and normal again. "What a fabulous book, Chloe! Sophie most certainly hasn't got this one. The photos are really lovely." She turned to Sophie. "What do you say to Chloe for giving you such a super present, Sophie?"

"Thank you," mumbled Sophie, so you could hardly hear her.

"Look at Chloe, please Sophie, and speak clearly."

Sophie raised her eyes for a second and said, "Thank you," in a slightly louder voice. But she didn't sound very thankful.

"And I think you should say sorry, too." Sophie looked absolutely furious. "I'm waiting," said her mum, looking even crosser.

"Sorry," said Sophie, in a voice that Chloe could only just hear.

Then her mum put the television back on and went out.

"Books are no fun anyway," said Sophie, the moment her mum had left the room. "This rucksack is much better." And she put it on her back then stood on the settee and looked at herself in the mirror on the wall.

The excitement seemed to go out of the party after that, so they just carried on watching the video until it was time to go.

Sophie's mum came into the sitting room with her arms full of party bags. "There's a piece of cake and a little present for everyone," she said, back to her smiling self.

When her mother arrived to collect her, Chloe thanked Sophie's mum for the party then said goodbye to Jessica. On her way out of Sophie's gate she glanced back at the house. Someone was watching her from an upstairs window. It was Sophie.

Chloe waved, but Sophie just looked back at her, wearing the biggest scowl in the world.

❀ ❀ ❀

Chapter Eight

Later, Chloe, her mum, her dad and her big brother, Ben, all had fish and chips together. It was almost Chloe's bedtime and she was still quite full from the tea at Sophie's party. She just had enough room for a bit of fish and chips. She told her family all about the games at the party and all about what they'd had for tea. Most of all she told them about her new friend, Jessica.

"I really wanted her to come and stay

the night at our house, but she's got to go to her granny's," Chloe explained.

"Talking of staying the night, it's bedtime for you, young lady," said Chloe's mum.

"But first, I'd like to see this smart new bedroom of yours," said her dad. "I hear you've been moving the furniture around and having a big tidy-up!"

Chloe didn't really want her dad to see the chest of drawers against the wall. She just wished everyone would forget all about it. Every time she looked at the chest, she felt naughty.

"It's nothing much," she said. "You can look tomorrow if you want."

"Why not now? Come on. Let's go."

So Chloe and her dad went upstairs together. Chloe's steps were slow and heavy. She noticed a funny smell on the way up, but she was too busy thinking about the writing on the wall to pay much attention to a smell. When they got to her room she opened the door. The smell seemed to be even stronger. Her dad didn't seem to notice anything odd though. He was staring all around him. Then his eyes rested on the chest.

Oh no! thought Chloe.

"Nice, tidy room," said her dad. He stroked his chin thoughtfully. "I'm not so sure about the chest though. I think it might look better if I pushed it just a little to the left."

He started to go towards the chest. Chloe watched in horror. "No!" she cried out. "No! I like it exactly where it is!"

Her dad stopped in his tracks and looked carefully at Chloe's wide, frightened eyes. "It's only a chest, Chloe. What's all the fuss about?"

Chloe didn't know what to say. She couldn't tell a lie. She didn't dare to tell the truth. So she just stood there, still and silent as a statue. Her dad started moving the chest. Chloe covered her eyes. Any second now he'd start shouting with rage.

She waited. Nothing happened. Chloe squeezed her eyes even more tightly shut. Her dad must be so furious he was speechless. Chloe waited again, then in the end she just had to have a tiny peek.

Cautiously she moved her hands away from her eyes and then she squinted through one eye. That was funny. The chest had been moved but the wall seemed to be blank!

Chloe opened her eyes properly and stared. Where was the writing? She looked at her dad. He didn't look cross. He just looked like his normal self.

"Your mum found a message on the wall, so she thought she'd better paint over it," explained her dad.

Of course. That was the funny smell – wet paint.

"Isn't Mum cross?" asked Chloe in a quivery voice.

"When she first saw what the chest was hiding, she was furious. I came home from football to find her going absolutely hopping mad."

"But why isn't she cross with me now, then?"

"Ask her yourself. Here she is."

Chloe's mum had come quietly into the bedroom.

"I'll tell you why I'm not cross, Chloe. It was because I suddenly thought that if I carried on being in a big temper, I might do something silly. Just like you did." Chloe went red. She felt even more ashamed of her temper now. Her mum carried on. "So I made myself calm down. And once I'd calmed down I realised that you must have been feeling very angry with yourself to have spoilt your bedroom wall like that. And I wondered what on earth could have made you so upset. I didn't think it could be just the drawing."

"It was because I'm useless at everything," said Chloe in a small voice. "I can't play the recorder. I can't even draw a horse. I'll never have a best friend when I'm not good at anything."

"I thought you told me you'd made a

new friend at the party. What was her name? Jessica?"

"Yes, I know. But I don't expect she'll stay friends with me for long when she realises that I'm no good at anything."

"Ssh!" said Chloe's dad, interrupting. His face wore a look of concentration.

"What?" asked Chloe's mum.

"Listen… What's that?"

They all three listened.

"It sounds like a recorder being played," said Chloe's mum.

"Exactly. And it's coming from Mrs Baxter's house," said her dad. "I didn't think Mrs Baxter was a recorder player."

Chloe went across to her window and opened it. She peered right round and could just see the upstairs side window of Mrs Baxter's house. It was open and someone was standing right by it. Chloe gasped. It was Jessica, with Chloe's recorder in her mouth.

✿ ✿ ✿

Chapter Nine

Chloe shouted out and waved vigorously.

"Jessica! Over here!"

Jessica stopped playing and looked out of the window.

"Chloe! What are you doing there?" she said with a huge smile.

"I live here. But what are you doing THERE? That's Mrs Baxter's house."

"She's not Mrs Baxter. She's my Granny B."

Chloe couldn't believe her ears. The

two girls were silent for a moment, then they both burst out laughing.

"You mean Mrs Baxter is your granny?" said Chloe happily.

Jessica nodded. She was still wearing the biggest smile in the world. "It's brilliant," she said. "We can see each other every time I stay with my granny. And now we've moved, that will be loads of times."

Chloe's mum was right behind her.

"Ask your granny if you can come over to our house for a little while," she called to Jessica. "Better still, ask Granny to come too."

"Cool! Thanks!" Jessica shouted back happily. Then she closed the window and disappeared in a flash.

Less than five minutes later, Chloe, her

mum, her dad, Jessica and Mrs Baxter were sitting in Chloe's living room.

The grown-ups were talking about what an incredible coincidence it was that Mrs Baxter turned out to be Jessica's granny. Mrs Baxter never stopped smiling.

"I'm so pleased that Jessica has got a friend living right next door. Now I know she'll come and visit me lots and lots."

Suddenly Jessica started giggling.

"What are you giggling about?" asked her granny.

"I'm just remembering something that happened at Sophie's party," spluttered Jessica.

"What happened at Sophie's party?" asked Ben, coming into the room at that very moment.

"Sophie was being bossy all through and Chloe did a brilliant imitation of her," explained Jessica. "Nobody else heard her – only me."

"Come on then, Chloe. Show us," said Ben, grinning at Chloe.

So Chloe stood up, put her hands on her waist, stuck her nose in the air and in her poshest, bossiest voice said, "You can look, but you can't touch."

Immediately everyone cracked up laughing, and went on and on for ages. Mrs Baxter was laughing so much she had tears rolling down her face. It was Ben who recovered first.

"You're pretty good at that, you know," he said to Chloe.

"I think she's absolutely brilliant at it," said Jessica. "I wish I could do something as well as that. I'm not much good at anything really."

"Everybody's good at something," said

Chloe's mum. "But sometimes we can't see it ourselves. We need a friend to point it out to us."

Chloe and her mum smiled at each other.

"Can we go up to my room for a bit," asked Chloe, happily.

"Yes, of course you can," said her mum. "But Chloe, the paint is still wet on your wall, so…"

Chloe wondered what her mum was going to say. She would never have guessed. Her mum put her hands on her waist, stuck her nose in the air, and in a bossy voice said, "You can look, but you can't touch."

The grown-ups were still laughing away as Chloe and Jessica went upstairs.

When the two girls were in Chloe's bedroom, Jessica said, "Do you know what my best friend used to call me at my other school?"

Chloe shook her head.

"Jess."

"That's a great name," said Chloe.

"Do YOU want to call me Jess now?" asked Jessica.

Chloe nodded. She was too happy to speak. It looked as though her wish was coming true.

✿ ✿ ✿